Angela McAllister took a degree in Humanities at Middlesex Polytechnic, and in the late 1970s started illustrating poetry anthologies, cookery books such as *Delia Smith's Christmas*, and other non-fiction. Since 1982 she has written over 30 books for children, some of which she also illustrated. Among her books are *The Snow Angel* (Bodley Head), *The Ice Palace* (Hutchinson), illustrated by Angela Barrett, *Jack and Lily* (Orion) and *Be Good, Gordon* (Bloomsbury). *The Wind Garden* (Bodley Head) was shortlisted for the Smarties Prize in 1994.

Jonathan Heale studied typography and fine art at the Royal College of Art. He now works in oils as well as woodcuts, and his hand-painted china is greatly sought after. His books include *The Ugly Duckling* and *The Steadfast Tin Soldier*, both written by Adrian Mitchell (Dorling Kindersley), and *Lamb Shenkin* and *Tibber*, both by William Mayne (Walker Books). *Lady Muck*, which William Mayne also wrote (Egmont), won the 1997 Kurt Maschler Award.

To Harvey – A.M.
To all fellow tortoises – J.H.

First published in Great Britain in 2001 and in the USA in 2004
by Frances Lincoln Children's Books, 4 Torriano Mews,
Torriano Avenue, London NW5 2RZ.

www.franceslincoln.com

Distributed in the USA by Publishers Group West.

British Library Cataloguing in Publication Data available on request.

The artwork for this book was done in watercolour and woodcuts.
Set in Perpetua.

ISBN 13:978-1-84507-142-4

Printed in Singapore

5 7 9 8 6

The Tortoise and the HARE

AN AESOP'S FABLE

Retold by Angela McAllister

With woodcuts by Jonathan Heale

F
FRANCES LINCOLN
CHILDREN'S BOOKS

One day, Tortoise overheard Hare boasting

to some rabbits.

"I can run so fast, I leave the wind behind,"

said Hare.

The rabbits were amazed.

"What nonsense," said Tortoise, creeping out of the rhubarb. "I'll give you a race."

Hare peered down at Tortoise. "Short, slow people aren't worth racing," he said, and he leapt right over the rhubarb.

The rabbits cheered.

Tortoise squinted up at Hare. "Think you can beat me, eh?"

"Right," said Hare. "I'll race you to the hedge and back."

"That's not far enough," said Tortoise. "We'll race down the lane, past the mill and across the meadow to the bridge."

So it was agreed.

Hare bounded off down the lane. Tortoise started to creep along, slow but sure.

Hare soon reached the mill. In the miller's garden he spied a row of carrots.

"Old wrinkly won't be coming by for hours," he said. "I've got plenty of time for elevenses."

He helped himself to the juiciest carrot.

Tortoise plodded down the lane.

He knew very well that Hare liked carrots

more than anything ...

Hare enjoyed his meal, then continued on his way.

The midday sun was hot. When he reached the meadow he felt full and sleepy.

"Old baggy-drawers will be miles behind," he said, with a yawn. "There's plenty of time for a nap." He settled down in the shade of a tree and went to sleep.

When Tortoise reached the mill, there were carrot tops lying scattered on the ground. Tortoise smiled and carried on his way, slow but sure.

When he came to the meadow, Tortoise tiptoed silently past Hare. Hare twitched an ear, then went on sleeping. Tortoise was tired and hot, but he didn't stop. He just crawled along, slow but sure.

All afternoon Tortoise trudged on through the grass.

Meanwhile, Hare dreamt he was leaping over the moon, while all the rabbits cheered.

The cheering woke him up.

To his surprise, he saw the rabbits

and other animals cheering loudly as

Tortoise struggled towards the bridge.

Hare realised he hadn't a moment to lose.

He bounded across the meadow – but was

too late. Tortoise lumbered on to the bridge

and the race was won!

Tortoise was exhausted. Hare felt a fool.

"I see I am fast, but not very wise," said Hare. "I promise not to boast any more."

The rabbits cheered again.

"Quite right," said Tortoise, with a yawn. "And now, how about carrying me home? One of us champions needs a nap!"